LOTTA
ON
TROUBLEMAKER
STREET

LOTTA
ON
TROUBLEMAKER
STREET

ASTRID LINDGREN
Illustrated by Julie Brinckloe

Macmillan Publishing Company
New York

© 1963 Macmillan Publishing Company,
a division of Macmillan, Inc.
Translated from the Swedish by Gerry Bothmer
Illustrations copyright © 1984 Julie Brinckloe
Macmillan Publishing Company
866 Third Avenue, New York, N.Y. 10022
Collier Macmillan Canada, Inc.
Swedish edition: Lotta på Bråkmakargatan
© 1962 Astrid Lindgren, Stockholm
First American edition 1963, reissued 1984
Printed in the United States of America
10 9 8 7 6 5 4 3 2 1
Library of Congress Cataloging in Publication Data
Lindgren, Astrid, date.
Lotta on Troublemaker Street.
Translation of: Lotta på Bråkmakargatan.
Summary: Angry because everyone at home is so mean,
five-year-old Lotta takes her favorite toy and goes to
live in a neighbor's attic.
[1. Behavior—Fiction] I. Brinckloe, Julie, ill.
II. Title.
PZ7.L6585Lo 1984   [E]   83-25619
ISBN 0-02-759040-2

CONTENTS

Everyone Is Mean to Lotta

One morning, shortly after her fifth birthday, Lotta woke up on Troublemaker Street, angry from the very start. She had had a bad dream, and Lotta thought that what you dreamed was true.

"They hit my Bamsie," she cried, when

Mother came to see why she was sitting in bed making such a racket at eight o'clock in the morning.

"Who hit your Bamsie?" asked Mother.

"Jonas and Maria," said Lotta.

"Lotta dear, it must have been a dream," said Mother. "Jonas and Maria have gone off to school. They certainly didn't have time to hit Bamsie."

"But they did, even though they didn't have time. I saw them," said Lotta, cuddling poor Bamsie.

Lotta's Bamsie was a fat little pig that Mother had made of pink cloth and given to Lotta on her third birthday. Bamsie had been clean and pink then, but now he was dirty and looked like a real little pig. Even so, Lotta was convinced that Bamsie was really a bear and insisted on calling him Bamsie Bear.

"Ha, ha, it isn't a bear, it's a pig," Jonas kept on saying.

"You're just silly," said Lotta. "He *is* a bear!"

"That's what *you* think," laughed Jonas. "What I would like to know, Lotta, is whether you think he's a polar bear or a regular bear."

"I think he's a piggly bear," said Lotta. "That's what I think!"

Lotta loved her piggly bear. At night, he slept beside her; and when Jonas and

Maria weren't around, she talked to him a lot.

Lotta was convinced that Bamsie was lying on the pillow feeling hurt because Jonas and Maria had hit him. As she stroked him, she cried and said, "My poor Bamsie! I'm going to give Jonas and Maria a real licking for this."

Jonas, Maria, Lotta, Mother, and Daddy lived in a yellow house on Troublemaker Street. Every morning, Jonas and Maria went to school, and Daddy went to his office. Only Mother and Lotta stayed home. "I'm so glad that I have my little Lotta," Mother would say. "Otherwise, I'd be all alone in the house."

"Yes, you're very lucky to have me," Lotta would agree. "If you didn't, you'd be all alone in the house, and I'd feel sorry for you."

But Lotta didn't say that this morning, not when she was so angry. She just sat there pouting, and looking very cross. It was time to get dressed, and Mother brought the striped sweater that Grandmother had knitted for Lotta.

"Not that one," said Lotta. "It tickles and scratches."

"No, it doesn't," said Mother patiently. "Feel how soft and smooth it is."

"It tickles and scratches," said Lotta without touching it. "I want to wear my velvet dress."

Lotta had a light blue velvet dress that was her Sunday best. She wanted to wear it even though it was only Thursday, and a very ordinary Thursday at that.

"You can wear it on Sunday," said Mother. "Today, you'll wear this sweater."

"Then I'd rather go naked," said Lotta.

"Suit yourself," said Mother, and she went downstairs to the kitchen.

So Lotta stayed behind in the children's room, naked and furious. Well, not exactly naked–she was wearing an undershirt, a pair of panties, stockings, and shoes.

"But except for that, I'm naked," said Lotta to Bamsie. He was the only one she could talk to.

"Lotta, you can come down and drink your hot chocolate now," Mother called from the stairs.

"That's what *you* think," Lotta mumbled, and she just kept on sitting in the same position.

"Answer me, Lotta!" Mother called. "Do you want your hot chocolate or don't you?"

Now this was just what Lotta wanted. Mother would keep on coaxing Lotta to drink her hot chocolate, and Lotta

wouldn't answer. It gave her a good feeling not to answer when Mother called.

But Lotta really was hungry, and she did want her hot chocolate. So after a while, when she felt Mother had waited long enough, Lotta picked up Bamsie and went downstairs.

She walked very slowly, stopping on each step, so Mother wouldn't be too sure. Maybe she would drink her hot chocolate, and maybe she wouldn't.

"I'll see how I feel," she told Bamsie, as she marched into the kitchen.

8

"Hello, Lotta," said Mother.

Lotta only stood in the doorway and pouted. Mother must see that she hadn't stopped being angry–not yet.

Usually Mother and Lotta had breakfast together in the kitchen. It was always so gay and friendly there, and it looked so inviting now. The sun was shining through the window and on the table was Lotta's very own cup filled with hot chocolate. Next to the hot chocolate was a piece of toast, covered with red raspberry jam. Usually Lotta talked all the time, but now she didn't say a word. Mother sat there drinking her coffee and reading the paper. She didn't say anything, either.

Finally Lotta sighed and said, "Well, if you really want me to, Mother, I'll drink my hot chocolate."

"I'm not insisting at all," said Mother.

"And besides, you should get dressed first."

Before, Lotta had only been angry. Now she was furious! Here she was with nothing to wear except an awful old sweater that tickled and scratched, and now, no food, either! How badly they treated her!

"Bad Mother!" said Lotta and stamped one foot.

"Now, Lotta," said Mother. "That's enough. Go upstairs to your room and stay there until you are ready to be good again."

Lotta let out a howl that could be heard all the way over to Mrs. Berg's house. She stormed out through the kitchen door and up the stairs to the children's room, screaming the whole time.

Next door, Mrs. Berg shook her head

and said, "Poor little Lotta must have a
tummy ache!"

But Lotta didn't have a tummy ache. She was just very, very angry. She stomped both feet, thoroughly outraged. Suddenly she saw the striped sweater lying on a chair. It looked scratchier than ever. Lotta pushed the sweater onto the floor. Then she stopped. She became very quiet. Next to the sweater lay a pair of scissors. Lotta usually used them to cut out paper dolls. Now she took the scissors and slowly cut out a big hole in the sweater.

"That's what you get," said Lotta,

"because you tickle and scratch." She wiggled her hand through the hole, and frowned. How big the hole was and how terrible to see her whole hand stick out, where no hand was *supposed* to be! Suddenly Lotta was afraid.

"I'll say that a dog made this hole," she said to Bamsie. She held the sweater in front of her and looked at it for a long

time. Then she picked up the scissors and cut off one arm.

"I'll say that he also chewed it to pieces," she said. She held the sweater up, and looked at it again. Then she picked up the scissors and quickly cut off the other arm.

"What a bad, bad dog," said Lotta, shaking her head. But now Lotta really felt

afraid and a little bit sick inside, as well. She rolled the sweater into a ball and stuffed it into the wastepaper basket. She didn't want to see it any more.

"Lotta, have you decided to be good again?" Mother called from downstairs.

Lotta sniffled her nose stubbornly and said to herself, "Not in the least bit." She took Bamsie in her arms and hugged him close to her. "It serves them right, Bamsie," she mumbled. "They're all so mean to us."

Lotta knew this wasn't true, but if you had just cut your sweater to pieces, you did need something besides a dog to blame it on.

"Everybody is mean to us," said Lotta, stretching out her arms. "That's why I cut up things." She glanced over at the waste-paper basket. "Besides, it *was* a dog, any-way," she said quietly.

Lotta Moves Away from Home

A few minutes later, Mother had to go out to do the shopping. Before leaving, she came into the children's room and said, "Hurry up and be good again, Lotta. Put your sweater on and you can come to the store with me."

Lotta just loved to go to the store. But the sweater she was supposed to put on was now a rag in the wastepaper basket. No wonder Lotta let out a new howl that made Mrs. Berg next door shake her head and wonder all the more.

"What on earth is the matter with you, Lotta?" said Mother.

"Nothing," said Lotta. "Nothing at all."

"Well, if you are going to make trouble all day, I'll just have to go to the store alone. Your hot chocolate and toast are still on the table if you want them. I'll be back in a little while."

Mother left and Lotta sat down on the floor and cried her eyes out. This wasn't what she wanted.

Little by little, she quieted down. Then she began to think. She would probably

have to sit in this children's room all her life just because of that sweater. Everyone else would be going to the store and to school and to the office, having all kinds of fun, but she would have to sit alone, without any clothes, on the bedroom floor with Bamsie.

"Then we might as well move," said Lotta to Bamsie. That was an idea! Mother had said that Brigit, Mrs. Larson's maid, had moved because she wasn't happy at the Larsons'.

"And I'm not happy at the Nymans'," said Lotta. The Nymans were Mother and Father and Jonas and Maria . . . and Lotta herself, of course.

"The Nymans are mean," said Lotta. "It will serve them right if we move." She made up her mind to move right away. "We must hurry before Mother comes home," she said to Bamsie, "because otherwise it won't work."

Moving away wouldn't be as good if nobody noticed it. And Lotta wanted the Nymans to notice and to feel bad because she had gone. So she got a piece of paper and a pen and wrote a note to Mother. Jonas had taught her how to read and write. It was hard, but Lotta managed. She printed:

It meant: I have moved. Look in the waste-basket.

"When Mother looks in the wastebasket, she will know why we've moved," she told Bamsie.

So Lotta picked up Bamsie Bear and moved out, dressed exactly as she was, in her undershirt, a pair of pants, and her shoes and stockings. On her way, she remembered to stop in the kitchen and drink her hot chocolate. She took the toast and jam along and finished it in the hallway.

Where Is Lotta Going?

It's all right to move, thought Lotta, if you know where you're moving to. But she hadn't the faintest idea.

"I'll ask Mrs. Berg if I can live with her," she decided. She threw Bamsie over the fence between the Nymans' garden and Mrs. Berg's, and then climbed over herself. Scotty, Mrs. Berg's dog, barked when he saw them, but he didn't scare Lotta in the least. She walked right up and knocked on Mrs. Berg's kitchen door.

"Hello," she said. "May I live here?"

"Hello, Lotta," said Mrs. Berg, through the screen door. "I thought you lived at home with your mother and father."

"Yes, but I'm moving," said Lotta. "I don't like it at the Nymans'."

"Well, then, I can understand why you would want to move," said Mrs. Berg and she opened the door wide. "But don't you think you ought to put some more clothes on?"

"I don't get either food or clothes at the Nymans'," said Lotta, and she walked into the kitchen.

Mrs. Berg happened to knit sweaters, caps, and gloves to sell to people who couldn't knit themselves. She went over to a drawer and pulled out a striped sweater. She slipped it over Lotta's head. It was too big and hung down loose like a dress.

"How does it feel?" asked Mrs. Berg.

"Fine," said Lotta. "It doesn't tickle and scratch."

"That's fine," said Mrs. Berg.

23

"Yes, that *is* fine," said Lotta. Then she began to look around.

"Where are you going to put my bed?" she asked.

"That's the problem," said Mrs. Berg. "You know, Lotta, I really don't think you can live here. I don't have room for another bed."

"But I have to live someplace, Mrs. Berg."

Mrs. Berg thought for a while and then said, "I think you ought to live all by yourself."

"But I don't have a house," said Lotta.

"You can rent my junk-room attic," said Mrs. Berg.

In the farthest corner of Mrs. Berg's garden was a shed where Mrs. Berg kept her lawn mower, her rake, her shovel, two sacks of potatoes, some wood, and a bit of everything. On the second floor was an attic where she kept old furniture and other odds and ends. "It's only junk," Mrs. Berg would say.

Sometimes Jonas, Maria, and Lotta liked to sneak up the stairs to the junk room to look at all those dusty things. But Mrs. Berg would always catch them and call from her window, "No, you mustn't go up there!"

But now it was different. Mrs. Berg was actually sitting there, telling Lotta that she could rent her attic! Lotta laughed. "That's the best news I've heard in a long time," she said. "May I move in right away?"

"First, let's go and see what it looks like," said Mrs. Berg. So Lotta and Mrs. Berg went outside and climbed up to the attic together. Mrs. Berg shook her head when she saw it.

"You can't live in all this mess, Lotta."

"Of course I can," said Lotta. "This is wonderful! And it's so nice and warm."

"Almost too nice and warm," said Mrs. Berg, and she opened the little window to air the place out.

Lotta ran to the window and leaned out.

"Look! I can see the Nymans' house from here," she shouted.

"Yes, they have a lovely house and garden," said Mrs. Berg.

Lotta stuck her tongue out at the yellow

house and laughed. "I'm never going to live there again. I'm going to live right here all my life. And I already have the curtains," said Lotta, happily touching the red and white checkered curtains that hung at the window. "Now all I need is furniture."

"Do you want to fix it up all by yourself or shall I help you?" asked Mrs. Berg.

"You can help a little bit," said Lotta. "But I must do the deciding."

"Well, decide then," said Mrs. Berg. "What furniture do you want?"

Lotta gave Mrs. Berg a big grin. This was more fun than she had ever dreamed of. She should have moved away from home a long time ago!

"I would like that," said Lotta, pointing to a small chest of drawers.

"You're welcome to it," said Mrs. Berg.

"And I'll need chairs," said Lotta. "Do you have chairs?"

"Yes, but they're broken," said Mrs. Berg.

"That doesn't matter," said Lotta. "Now, let's see . . . what else? How about a bed? Do you have one?"

"Yes, I think so," said Mrs. Berg. "There's a small bed behind those packing cases and there's even a doll's bed somewhere. My daughter slept in it when she was little."

"In the doll's bed?" asked Lotta.

"No, in the child's bed, of course," said Mrs. Berg.

"Then I can sleep in it now," said Lotta. "And Bamsie can sleep in the doll's bed so he won't be so crowded. Do you have any bedclothes?"

"Yes, there is a mattress, some pillows,

and maybe a blanket," said Mrs. Berg. "But no sheets."

"I don't care about sheets," said Lotta. "Would you help me with the furniture, Mrs. Berg?"

Mrs. Berg obligingly pulled out the furniture and helped Lotta arrange the small room. They put the table and the chairs next to the window, and the chest of drawers against one wall and the bed against the other. They put the doll's bed next to the big bed and Lotta propped Bamsie up on the little pillow.

"It's just like a real room," Lotta exclaimed.

Mrs. Berg found an old strip of carpet, which she put on the floor. The carpet made it look even more like a real room. Next, Mrs. Berg put a round, fly-specked mirror over the chest. Above Lotta's bed she hung a picture of Little Red Riding Hood and the wolf. Lotta liked it.

"You're quite right–I must have pictures," she said. "Otherwise it isn't a real home. That's a pretty one, Mrs. Berg."

Lotta used to say that when she grew up, she would have corns on her toes like Mrs. Berg's and a *housebole* like her mother's. Now, as she looked around her little room, she felt very content. "I already have my *housebole*," she sighed.

"But don't be in too big a hurry about the corns," smiled Mrs. Berg.

"No, I guess they'll have to wait a while," said Lotta, and she sneezed three times in a row.

"It's awfully dusty in here," said Mrs. Berg. "That's why you're sneezing."

"I'll dust," said Lotta. "Do you have a dustcloth?"

"Look in the chest of drawers," said Mrs. Berg.

Lotta pulled out the top drawer. "Oh, my!" she said. "These are real doll's dishes!"

Mrs. Berg looked into the drawer. "Oh, yes, I had forgotten all about those doll's dishes."

"What luck that I found them!" said Lotta, and she unpacked the dishes on the table. They were white with small blue flowers. There were cups and saucers and a serving dish and a coffee pot, a sugar bowl and a cream pitcher. Lotta jumped up and down.

"If Maria saw this, she would go out of her mind," she laughed.

"I can hardly believe *that*," said Mrs. Berg, with a twinkle in her eyes. "Take a look and see if there is a dustcloth in one

of the other drawers."

Lotta pulled out the next drawer and found a big doll with blue eyes and black hair.

"Oh!" said Lotta. "Oh!"

"Well, well, there is Viola Lou," said Mrs. Berg.

"Is that her name?" said Lotta. "She is beautiful! Bamsie can't have the doll's bed

now because that's where Viola Lou is going to sleep. . . . Will you let me have her, Mrs. Berg?"

"Yes, if you take good care of her," said Mrs. Berg. "Of course she *will* have to sleep in her own bed, and Bamsie *will* have to move out."

Lotta nodded. "Yes. Besides, I think he'd really prefer to sleep with me."

"Try the bottom drawer," said Mrs. Berg.

"You'll probably find some doll's clothes there. I remember sewing such an awful lot of things for that doll."

Lotta pulled out the bottom drawer. It was filled with sweaters and dresses and coats and hats and underwear and night-gowns, all for Viola Lou.

"If Maria saw this, she would *really* go out of her mind," Lotta said again. She pulled all the clothes out of the drawer.

Then she sat down in the middle of the floor and began trying them on Viola Lou. Mrs. Berg found a torn towel and handed it to Lotta for her dusting. But Lotta shook her head.

"I can dust later, Mrs. Berg. Now I have to make up my mind which dress is going to be her Sunday best."

It was hard to pick the right dress—there were so many of them! There were red ones and yellow ones and blue and white ones and checkered ones and some that were dotted and some that were flowered.

"The white embroidered dress is going to be her best," said Lotta at last. "She will only be allowed to wear it on Sundays."

"You're absolutely right," said Mrs. Berg. "You mustn't let her wear it for every day."

Then Mrs. Berg stroked Lotta's cheek

and said, "Now that we've finished here, I think I'd better go home."

Lotta nodded. "All right, but you must come and visit me sometime. If you see the Nymans, tell them that I live in my own house now and that I'm never coming back again."

"I'll do that," said Mrs. Berg.

When she was halfway down the stairs, Lotta shouted, "Oh, Mrs. Berg, what about my food?"

"Yes, of course," said Mrs. Berg.

"Will you give me some?" asked Lotta.

"Yes, but you will have to come and get it yourself," said Mrs. Berg. "I don't feel like running up and down these stairs."

Just then, Lotta looked up and saw a basket that was hanging from a hook on the ceiling.

"Mrs. Berg," she called, "I have a wonderful idea!"

Lotta's idea was to tie a long string to the basket and lower it from the window so that Mrs. Berg could put food in it.

"Then I'll just pull it up and wham! There is the food!" said Lotta.

"You're a clever one," said Mrs. Berg. She laughed and went to get some food for Lotta. When she came back, Lotta had already lowered the basket.

"Wham! Here is the food," shouted Mrs. Berg.

"Don't tell me what I'm getting," called Lotta. "I want to be surprised."

She pulled up the basket and inside were an orangeade, two straws, a cold potato pancake wrapped in a piece of paper, and a small jar of jam.

"Better than at the Nymans'," said Lotta. "Good-by, Mrs. Berg, and thank you very much."

Mrs. Berg left, and Lotta put the pancake on the table and smothered it with jam. Then she rolled it up and held it with both hands and took big bites. In between, she drank the orangeade through the straws.

39

"Couldn't be better," said Lotta. "And no dishes! I wonder why people say it's so hard to keep house."

When she had finished eating, she wiped her fingers on the dustcloth. Then she dusted the furniture. She dusted the table, the chest of drawers, the chairs, the bed, the doll's bed, the mirror, and the picture of Little Red Riding Hood and the wolf. Then she made up Viola Lou's bed and the bigger bed for herself and Bamsie. Lotta was so happy about her *housebole* that she sang and hummed a song she had learned.

> *I come into my little house—*
>   *It's night*
>   *And dark*
>   *And I'm alone.*
> *I click on my yellow light.*
> *My cat purrs, "Welcome home."*

"But I don't have a cat," said Lotta, quietly.

Lotta Gets a Visitor

Lotta played happily with Viola Lou, Bamsie, and the doll's dishes for a long time. Then she dusted her furniture five more times, and then she sat down on a chair and began to think.

"What on earth do you do in a *house-hole* all day long?" she asked Bamsie.

But just then footsteps came pounding up the stairs. It was Jonas and Maria.

"I've moved," Lotta announced.

"Yes, we know," said Jonas. "Mrs. Berg told us."

"I'm going to live here all my life," said Lotta.

"That's what you think," said Jonas.

Maria had gone straight to the doll dishes.

"Oh!" was all she said as she tenderly picked up the cups, the serving dish, and the coffee pot. Then she saw Viola Lou and all her pretty clothes. "Oh!" she said again, and she began going through all the dresses to see how many there were.

"Don't touch them!" warned Lotta. "This is my house now, and these are my things."

"Won't you let me play with them for just a little while?" said Maria pleadingly.

"All right," Lotta consented. "But only for a little while."

After a moment, Lotta asked, "Is Mother crying?"

"Of course not," said Jonas.

"Of course I'm crying," said a voice from the stairs, and suddenly there stood Mother. "Of course I'm crying for my little Lotta."

Lotta looked very pleased. "I'm sorry, Mother," she said. "But I've moved now and have my own *househole* to keep up. It keeps me very busy."

"So I see," said Mother. "You have a very nice place here."

"Much better than at home," said Lotta, fluffing out the curtains.

"I brought you a plant. That's the custom when someone moves," said Mother, and she gave Lotta a potted begonia.

"How nice," said Lotta. "I'll put it on my windowsill. Thank you very much."

Lotta dusted all her furniture again so that Mother, Maria, and Jonas could watch her. They agreed that she was very good at keeping house.

When Lotta was through with her dusting, Mother asked, "Are you coming home for dinner with Jonas and Maria?"

"No, Mrs. Berg is giving me my food," said Lotta, and she showed them how cleverly the basket system worked.

"You're not so dumb after all," said Jonas, and he sat down on the floor and thumbed through some old magazines that he had found in a corner.

"Well, good-by, Lotta," said Mother. "If you should decide that you want to move back home around Christmas time, you know we'll be happy to have you."

"How much longer before Christmas?" Lotta wanted to know.

"Seven months," said Mother.

"Oh, I'll probably be living here longer than seven months," said Lotta.

"That's what you think," said Jonas and he laughed.

Mother left, and Lotta and Maria played with Viola Lou. Jonas sat on the floor reading his magazines.

"Isn't my place fun, Maria?" said Lotta.

"It's the best playhouse I've ever seen."

"It isn't a playhouse," said Lotta. "It's my *real* home."

Suddenly, heavy footsteps came up the stairway. It was Daddy.

"I've heard some bad news," he said. "People around town are saying that you've moved away from home, Lotta. Is it true?"

Lotta nodded. "Yes, I have."

"This is going to be a very sad night for

me, Lotta. Just think how bad I'll feel when I come into the children's room to say good night.... There will be your empty bed. My Lotta will be gone!"

"It can't be helped," said Lotta firmly.

"Poor Daddy," Lotta sighed to herself. She really felt sorry for him.

"No, I guess it can't be helped," said Daddy. "Jonas and Maria, you'd better come home now, we're having hamburgers and stewed apricots for supper."

"Good-by, Lotta dear," said Daddy as he went downstairs.

"Good-by," said Lotta.

"So long," said Jonas and Maria.

"So long," said Lotta, and she went to the window to wave good-by.

It's Night and I'm Alone

Lotta was alone. Mrs. Berg brought her some dinner, and Lotta hauled it up in the basket. There was another orangeade, two straws, and a cold pork chop.

"Just as good as at the Nymans'," said Lotta, and she offered a bite to Bamsie.

After she had eaten, she dusted her fur-

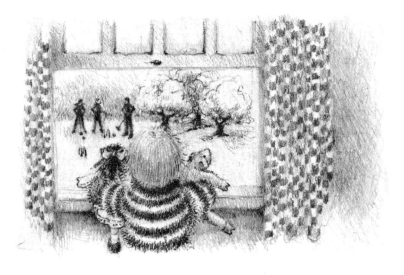

niture again. Then she went to the window and watched the Nymans in their backyard. Jonas and Maria were playing croquet with Daddy. The apple trees were in bloom and they looked like big bunches of flowers. It was a very pretty sight.

"Croquet is fun," said Lotta to Bamsie, "but not as much fun as keeping your own house."

It began to get dark, and Daddy, Jonas, and Maria went inside their warm yellow house. Lotta sighed. Now she didn't have anything more to look at.

While she had been looking out the window, something had happened in Mrs. Berg's attic—something Lotta hadn't planned on. It had gotten dark. The darkness had settled in the nooks and in the corners and it looked very black. It crept closer and closer to Lotta and filled the room until there was only one small spot of light over where the window was.

"We'd better go to bed, Bamsie. Soon we won't be able to see a thing," said Lotta.

She quickly tucked Viola Lou into the doll's bed and bedded Bamsie down in her own. Then she crawled in beside him and pulled the covers up over her head.

"It's not that I'm afraid of the dark," Lotta said, "it's just very sad. Besides, I'm sleepy."

She sighed deeply. A couple of times, she sat up and looked out into the dark. Then she shivered and crawled down under her blanket again, hugging Bamsie closer than ever.

"By this time, Jonas and Maria are probably in bed, too," she said. "And Mother and Daddy will be coming in to say good night to them. But not to me...."

She sighed again, and she noticed that her sigh was the only sound in the attic; otherwise, all was still.

"It shouldn't be so very, very quiet," thought Lotta. So she started to sing her song again.

> *I come into my little house—*
> *It's night*
> *And dark*
> *And I'm alone.*

Then Lotta stopped. Her voice was quavering. She tried again:

I come into my little house—
It's night
And dark
And I'm alone.

But Lotta couldn't sing any more. She broke into sobs. Then she heard Daddy's heavy footsteps on the stairs, and he was singing.

I click on my yellow light.
My cat purrs, "Welcome home."

Lotta sat up in bed. "Daddy, if I only had a cat," she sobbed.

Daddy picked Lotta up and held her in his arms.

"You know, Lotta, Mother is so sad. Don't you think you'll be able to come home before Christmas?"

"I want to move back right now," said Lotta.

So Daddy took Lotta and Bamsie up in his arms and carried them back to the yellow house and to Mother.

"Lotta has moved back home!" Daddy called out as they came into the front hall-way.

Mother was sitting in front of the fire in the living room. She stretched out her arms to Lotta and smiled. "Is it true? Have you really moved back home, Lotta?"

Lotta threw herself into her mother's arms and cried so hard that the tears streamed down her face.

"I'm going to live with you all my life, Mother," she sobbed.

"That's wonderful," said Mother.

Lotta curled up in Mother's lap and didn't say a word for a long time. Finally,

through her sniffles, she said, "Mother, I
have another striped sweater. Mrs. Berg
gave it to me. Is that all right?"

Mother didn't answer. She just sat there
quietly looking at Lotta. Then Lotta
lowered her eyes and mumbled, "I cut the
other one to pieces and I want to say that
I'm sorry, but it's very hard."

"What if I say I'm sorry, too?" said Mother.

"Then we can say I'm sorry together," said Lotta.

She threw her arms around her mother's neck and squeezed her as hard as she could.

"I'm sorry, I'm sorry, I'm sorry, I'm sorry," she said.

So Mother carried Lotta and Bamsie up to the children's room and tucked them into their own comfortable bed, with clean sheets and a pink blanket that Lotta used to pick fluffy bits out of when she was falling asleep.

Daddy came upstairs, too, and both Mother and Daddy kissed Lotta good night and said, "Good night, dear little Lotta."

Then they went back downstairs.

"They are so nice," said Lotta to Bamsie.

Jonas and Maria were almost asleep, but Jonas woke up enough to say, "I knew you'd be too scared to stay over there all night."

"I've decided to stay there in the daytime, instead, and play and keep my *househole,* so there!" said Lotta. "And if you and Maria hit Bamsie again, I'm going to have to give you both a licking!"

"Hit Bamsie? We never touched your old piggly bear." Jonas laughed and fell asleep.

But Lotta lay awake for a little while, singing her song to herself:

> *I come into my little house–*
> > *It's night*
> > *And dark*
> > *And I'm alone.*
> *I click on my yellow light.*
> *My cat purrs, "Welcome home."*

"But that song isn't about me any more. That's about another Lotta," said Lotta to Bamsie. Then she hugged him tight and fell fast asleep.